My dear Aunt Moonbeam,

It was wonderful to see everyone in Weavewillow, although I wish the circumstances had been a bit better. Battling goblins was not my idea of a grand homecoming, but at least we won the day, and for the moment, everything is quiet.

When I was home, I noticed that Mother had nailed your copy of A Practical Guide to Dragons on the wall of our house. How thrilling to see it there! Ever since I set off again, I've been thinking of more amazing and useful knowledge I could share with you about dragons and their kind. I have learned so much more since I wrote that tome. After all, I have spent time with a gold dragon. I have ridden on his back and had many amazing adventures by his side.

It seems no matter where I travel, I meet fellow wanderers who are enthralled by my stories of how one goes about finding, raising, and training a dragon. One day I will return home to tell these tales around the hearth, but for now I'm having too much fun on my adventures. And so until then, I'm sending you this new book filled with everything I know. Perhaps you can share it with my cousins so that when the time comes for them to set out, their adventures will be as thrilling as my own.

Long live dragons!

Sindri
Written overlooking the shores of the Sirrion Sea, 356 AC

A Practical Guide to
Dragon Riding

Inscribed by

Sindri Suncatcher

The Greatest Kender Wizard
Who Ever Lived

MIRRORSTONE™

DRAGON BASICS

en different types of dragons roam the world. Our legends tell us that all the dragons of simple colors are generally evil, while all the dragons of shimmery, metallic colors are good. If you wish to find a dragon to train and ride, you must become familiar with these dragons and where they live. Learn which treasures appeal to each dragon too. After all, dragons are very intelligent creatures. A gift might endear the dragon to you, or if you come across a surly dragon, it may even save your life!

I prefer not to judge a dragon by the color of its skin. My friends tell me this is foolish, but I can't see why we should make assumptions about any living creature. I have known (and caught a ride on) a blue dragon. He was rather surly, but once I regaled him with my tales, he was more than willing to give me a ride.

Body

All dragons share some basic traits. Each and every one has a magnificent pair of wings. A long, tapered tail helps the dragon to balance, to battle, and to fly. Four powerful legs launch the dragon into the skies. A dragon's tongue and its nose work together to smell prey, and a dragon's eyesight is exceptional.

Blue

Red

Black

White

Green

Gold

Bronze

Silver

Copper

Brass

Habitat

Five kinds of dragons make their homes in mountainous regions. You're more likely to meet a red or copper dragon on a hot, dry mountain trail, while you may find yourself face-to-face with a white or silver atop a cold, high peak. Blue and brass dragons may cross your path while you trek through desert regions, and you may meet a bronze dragon resting on a tropical beach. Black dragons make their homes in boggy swamps, green dragons prefer forests, and gold dragons will nest anywhere with a secluded lair.

Of course, A Practical Guide to Dragons catalogs each dragon's specific habitat, treasure, anatomy, and diet in detail, should you find yourself wanting more information.

Treasure

All dragons hoard treasure. Blacks collect coins. Bronze dragons are drawn to pearls and gold. And red dragons will amass just about anything of value. Gemstones and jewelry catch the eyes of silver, blue, and white dragons. The vengeful green dragon likes to hoard souvenirs from its victories in battle, while the more refined gold and copper dragons prefer fine art. The least demanding of all is the brass dragon, who enjoy finely woven garments.

Raising a Dragon

More mature dragons have softened a bit, and they might be more willing to form a relationship with you.

If you want to learn to ride a dragon, the first step is to find one. Always remember: Most dragons will not want to be trained by you. After all, why would they? Dragons are spectacular creatures, and they do just fine on their own. They are also very confident, especially the younger ones.

If you are in need of a dragon to train and ride, one of the first questions you should ask the dragon is its age. The dragon's age will help you determine if the dragon will be willing to work with you.

If you can convince a dragon to let you ride it, you must understand that the dragon is forming a partnership with you. You will not necessarily be the one in control. The younger a dragon is, the more independent and inflexible it might be. It can turn from friend to enemy in an instant.

Unless the world is in peril. Then the good dragons will fight side by side with us, no matter their age.

Great Wyrm

Adult

Young Adult

Wyrmling

Finding a Dragon

If an older dragon will not agree to a partnership with you, what should you do? Why, you should raise the dragon yourself, of course! In order to care for and hatch a dragon egg, you must first find one. And that, my friends, is the challenge. Dragon mothers don't just leave their eggs lying around for all to see. The eggs are well hidden, usually buried beneath the ground or within a pile of leaves.

A telltale sign of a dragon's nest is often a mound or something unusual to that terrain. Beware! Approaching a dragon's nest is very dangerous. The dragon mother usually watches over her nest, as might the dragon father. Most dragon parents are very dedicated to their offspring. You must be patient, cunning, and very brave if you wish to take an egg from a dragon's nest. Although dragon mothers lay several eggs, she might notice if one is missing. It is best if you can find a nest that has been abandoned for some reason. Observing the nest over several days will help you determine the best way to approach it.

A Dragon Mother's Wrath

Never underestimate a dragon mother's wrath. If you do choose to steal a dragon egg, proceed with extreme caution. For the most part, dragons, whether chromatic or metallic, maintain a patient outlook on life. Because their lives last thousands of years, they seldom encounter a problem that requires urgent attention. But there is one exception. If ever someone threatens a dragon's life, its mate, or its offspring, a dragon will leap to defend itself and its family at all costs. Pity the adventurer who is caught daring to slip away with a dragon egg. No amount of talking, pleading, or I dare say even combat, will save the situation. A dragon mother will never part with her eggs willingly and will fight ceaselessly to save them.

Don't think that a simple sword can help you defeat dragon parents. They have overlapping scales that are difficult to penetrate, like a suit of armor.

Don't try to steal an egg at night. Dragons can see well even in darkness. The dragon mother will probably see you before you will see her!

Do you recognize this habitat? What kind of dragon mother is this? What kind of dragon egg, then, would this be? This is important! Raising a chromatic dragon can be much trickier than raising a metallic one!

Stay far away from these sharp teeth.

This map shows several dragon habitats and the nests for their eggs.

Can you find them all?

DRAGONS AND THEIR NESTS

Black: Under boggy marshes

Blue: Buried in hot sand

Red: On top of mountain

Green: Buried in leaves

White: Encased in ice on mountaintops

Brass: Buried in open flame in sand

Bronze: In cave near the sea

Copper: Buried in cool clay on mountains

Silver: Encased in snow on high peak

Gold: Anywhere, in open flame

Hatching the Eggs

Once you have located an egg, you must handle it very carefully. In order for your egg to hatch, it must be kept in certain conditions. You can't simply bury the egg in the ground like a seed and hope a healthy, happy dragon will hatch from it. You must duplicate the same conditions in which you found the egg. Otherwise, the dragon inside will not develop fully.

While going through Maddoc's study one day, I came across this useful pamphlet about dragon eggs. It was written by a wizard who spent many years raising orphaned dragons.

Remember, you can't predict the exact date of an egg's hatching because you don't know the day it was laid, only the day you stole it. At that point, it could be newly laid or just about to hatch!

Maddoc was my old mentor, but we have since parted ways.

Brass Dragon

My experience has proven that the best way to incubate a brass dragon egg is with an oven or an ongoing fire. The egg must be kept within a flame for at least 480 days. Only with constant and fierce heat will the egg hatch a healthy wyrmling.

Bronze Dragon

As far as I can observe, the only place to hatch a bronze dragon egg is near the sea. The egg must remain close to the fumes of the salty tide, but the nest is normally in a dry cave. Total incubation time is 600 days.

Copper Dragon

This egg has two methods of care. The first (recommended) is to keep the egg firmly covered by cool sand or clay. The other option is to place the egg in strong acid. Be sure to check on your egg after 540 days.

Gold Dragon

From what I can determine, the same instructions apply here as for the brass dragon. You must keep the egg over an open flame or in a hot oven. A gold dragon will hatch after 720 days.

Silver Dragon

If you wish to hatch a silver dragon, you must reside in a very cold place. Your dragon egg must be buried in the snow or encased in ice. Eggs in temperatures greater than zero degrees will not hatch. If you are successful, the egg will hatch in about 660 days.

Black Dragon

The best place for this egg to incubate is deep within a swamp, bog, or marsh. Or, if you happen to have strong acid lying around, you might also place the egg within a jar. Waiting time: 480 days.

Blue Dragon

Whereas most dragon eggs can be left unattended for several days, this egg must be constantly observed. I have experimented with many different blue dragon eggs, and I have reached this conclusion: Half of the day, the egg must be kept in a very hot place, between 90 and 120 degrees. The other half of the day, the egg must be placed in a cooler place, between 40 and 60 degrees. This process continues for 600 days.

Fahrenheit

Green Dragon

The green dragon's egg is one of the easiest to care for. Green dragon eggs can be buried beneath the soil, preferably wrapped in leaves soaked by rainwater. If you would rather keep the egg inside, then it must sit in strong acid. The green dragon egg takes 480 days to hatch.

Red Dragon

I have determined that this egg must be kept in fire or in an area that is constantly 140 degrees. However, I would not advise a volcano, since the parents might be lurking about. Incubation time is about 660 days.

White Dragon

Like the silver dragon, the egg of a white dragon must be kept in snow or ice, and it must not be in temperatures above zero degrees. This egg takes the shortest time to hatch—only 420 days.

Caring for a Wyrmling

Once you become the proud adoptive parent of a dragon wyrmling, the real challenge begins. Taking care of a dragon wyrmling is not an easy feat. Even though your dragon is newly hatched, it still has many of the characteristics of an adult dragon.

Here are some more comments from the wizard who wrote about dragon eggs.

After having studied the behavior of numerous wyrmlings, I have made the following observations:

1. Most wyrmlings are ready to fly one hour after hatching.

2. The wyrmling's first act is one of survival: finding food. To meet this need, it eats its own eggshell. It is helpful if the adoptive parents have some traditional dragon food on hand as well.

3. Most wyrmlings next begin to explore their environment. I believe this is because they are looking for a safe lair to call home.

4. Wyrmlings recognize their own kind, and that is whom they turn to for guidance. They view any creature that is not a dragon with suspicion.

5. Dragon wyrmlings are born with a sense of their importance in the world. Although they are not aware of all their powers, they are born with confidence. It has been my experience that they truly do look down upon creatures that are not dragons like they are.

Conclusion: Because a dragon wyrmling already believes itself to be superior to you, you must convince your wyrmling that you are needed and on its level.

The wyrmling's wings are fully
formed, but they are much smaller
than the body. This will slowly
change as the wyrmling grows.

The wyrmling's
head is also large
compared to its body.

The wyrmling can hatch from the egg on
its own. It breaks the egg from the inside.
If a parent is nearby, it can help.

Wyrmlings and Young Dragons

Wyrmlings and young dragons are adorable! But don't let them fool you. Wyrmlings and young dragons are still dragons. They have a dragon's cunning and intelligence, although neither is fully developed. Wyrmlings are often more dangerous than adult dragons because they tend to be more selfish. They do not think through their actions. And the last thing they want to do is listen to someone who is not a dragon.

Brass Wyrmling

Young brass dragons love to chatter. Talk, talk, talk. They'll talk to anyone, whether the other being talks back or not. In fact, if no one stops to talk to the wyrmling, it will talk to itself.

Pay attention! Talking and listening to your brass dragon wyrmling is one way to ensure that the wyrmling will bond to you! Brass dragons are very social creatures.

When a bronze wyrmling hatches, it appears more yellow
than bronze, with a green hue lining the tips of its wings.
As the wyrmling grows older, the yellow will turn a rich
shade of bronze.

Bronze Wyrmling

Think about a playful puppy or kitten, and you understand what a
bronze dragon wyrmling is all about. The bronze wyrmling enjoys
frolicking with other animals, especially those that live along the
bronze dragon's habitat—a rocky coast. The wyrmling will also
help creatures in need. It is not particularly fond of humans who
hunt or fish, so these should not be one of your pastimes if you
choose to raise a bronze dragon wyrmling.

Aha! Perhaps if you help the bronze
wyrmling help others, your wyrmling
will be more inclined to help you!

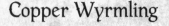

Copper Wyrmling

This wyrmling loves a challenge, usually of the mental kind. A riddle, a pun, a silly poem—anything that challenges the wyrmling's intellect is certain to keep the wyrmling near you. The copper wyrmling loves to unravel mysteries, so it might wander from your side to discover something new. The wyrmling also enjoys physical challenges such as a quick clash of swords or a hunt for small creatures to eat, like spiders and centipedes.

You need to stay sharp and keep on your toes for this little bugger!

Note that when a gold wyrmling hatches, it lacks the tentacle whiskers and horns that distinguish an adult gold dragon. As the wyrmling matures and it takes on these adult traits, be sensitive to your wyrmling's mood. Some wrymlings become cranky during this time for the horns and whiskers can cause pain as they grow in.

Silver Wyrmling

You will soon discover that this wyrmling is constantly under your feet. That's because silver dragon wyrmlings find humans fascinating. They always want to know why humans act as they do or perform certain tasks. This wyrmling also has an insatiable need to help people, and it will change form as needed to lend assistance. Satisfying this wyrmling's curiosity is one way to form a bond with it.

It might even change into a kender!

Silver dragons love to fly so if you choose to train a silver wyrmling, prepare to spend hours soaring through the skies!

Gold Wyrmling

A gold wyrmling makes an excellent candidate for a human companion because often the wyrmling's parents will send it off to be fostered by another family. It may sound harsh, but not only does fostering protect the young gold dragon, but it helps it learn about the world. If the gold dragon is fostered by a human family, it often takes the form of a human child. But don't be fooled! The child still has the superior intelligence of a gold dragon wyrmling.

Interesting, don't you think? Look around you. A gold dragon wyrmling might be among your friends!

Black Wyrmling

A young black dragon is a fierce creature, to be sure! The black dragon wyrmling, which lives in the swamp, believes it is the most evil and dangerous creature around. It spits acid at anything that moves— and even things that don't move! So watch out for this little spitfire if you want to be its mentor!

For many months after birth, a black wyrmling's scales will be tiny, delicate, and shiny. Over time, the scales grow and thicken, and its hide turns a dull shade of black.

Temper, temper! The black dragon wyrmling is always angry about something!

Of all the chromatics, this dragon might be your best bet to train.

Blue Wyrmling

A blue dragon wyrmling is not quite as ferocious as a black, although it loves to hunt. It spends the day and night soaring across the desert, looking for prey. You might mistake it for a large bird or a bat. But don't be surprised if it comes down and swoops in on your meal! It will probably try to bully you away from it.

Red Wyrmling

You might get burned with this one, my friends! Red dragon wyrmlings love to play with fire. They especially enjoy burning things that people have made. They'll fly above a town and shoot flames just to cause destruction. You'll need to keep its fiery tendencies under control if you wish to train a red dragon wyrmling.

The red dragon wyrmling also likes a good game of cat and mouse. Can you guess who the mouse would be?

If you plan to train a blue dragon, be sure you like hot weather! A blue prefers to fly when the sun shines and the temperature has reached the peak of the day.

Green Wyrmling

Don't let a green dragon wyrmling hear you giggle! These wyrmlings despise anything fun or silly. They'll stalk through the forest, looking for forest folk having a good time, then swoop down and destroy their party. So if you choose to train a green dragon, you'd better not laugh! The bonding process will be extremely compromised if you do.

Make certain your green wyrmling remains well fed at all times. Otherwise you may find your green dragon gobbling up any unsuspecting food source in its path. Green dragons will eat anything if they are hungry enough, from trees and other plants to elves and sprites!

Even kender are not safe from a green dragon's voracious appetite!

When a green dragon hatches, you may worry that you stole a black dragon's eggs by mistake! But do not fear. All green dragons have a black hide when they first emerge from their eggs. As the dragon matures its scales slowly fade to a glossy shade of green.

White Wyrmling

Unless you are in the snowy regions of the world, you might not come across a white dragon wyrmling. But in case you do, watch out that it doesn't mistake you for a big animal of prey, such as a polar bear or a walrus. Even though the wyrmling may be small, it loves to attack larger prey, so keep your head up!

Think twice before you decide to train a white dragon wyrmling. You'll have to bundle up, that's for sure!

Naming Your Wyrmling

To initiate the bond you wish to form with your wyrmling, be sure to name it. Choose a name that is magical and majestic, one that when spoken commands respect, that people will say with awe. Give your wyrmling a name it will be proud of!

Suggested Names

Black dragon	Blight
Blue dragon	Dazzle
Brass dragon	Poccri
Bronze dragon	Immersa
Copper dragon	Snydel
Gold dragon	Luminia
Green dragon	Blister
Red dragon	Scorch
Silver dragon	Karaglen
White dragon	Rime

TRAINING A DRAGON

Once your wyrmling has grown to the size of a horse and is strong enough to carry you on its back, you may begin training it to become your mount. It takes a very special person to ride a dragon, mostly because a dragon will not let just anyone ride it. If you wish to be a dragon rider, you must:

- Have a love and respect of other creatures.
- Be strong of mind.
- Be able to concentrate.
- Know how to fall (for you just might take a tumble from the back of your dragon).
- Have no fear of heights. Your dragon will take you higher than you've ever flown before.

Here is a note from my journal the first time I ever attempted to ride a dragon.

The first time I climbed on a dragon's back is one of my favorite memories. Auren's gold scales were smooth and sleek, and his body was warm. I could feel him shift slightly beneath me as I climbed onto his scales, and I wondered idly if I could hold on without a saddle. But it didn't matter. Auren shot through the doorway and down a tunnel, and the wind overtook me as I clung to his scales. Then, before I knew it, we burst out of the cliffside and into the sky. My heart was racing with elation, and I looked at the sea below us in awe. Auren's wings made a soft thwump, thump sound as they beat on either side of me. Rizzek clung to me, fearing he might fall, but Auren flew true, and I drank up the sight of a storm swirling above the haunted sea.

Gearing Up

When riding a dragon, you will not be riding directly on the dragon's back. That would not be a very secure ride! Instead, you will sit in a saddle especially designed for dragons to wear. Because dragons are such independent creatures, your dragon might not enjoy the feel of the saddle strapped around its middle. However, your dragon will recognize that the saddle will keep you safe. Because of the strong bond you share, your dragon will soon realize the saddle's importance.

Note that the saddle has no place in which to secure your legs and feet. This is so you can grab hold of the dragon with your legs. You can also wrap your feet around the straps, if needed.

To ride a dragon, you do not use reins as you would with a horse. You do not steer a dragon, but rather you and the dragon work together to decide where to go. You can issue commands, of course, but in most circumstances, you and the dragon will think as one. Together, you and the dragon are unbeatable!

The strap should fit snugly—but not tightly—around the dragon, just above the wings.

Make Your Own Dragon Saddle

Dragon saddles are not easy to come by. Unless you know someone who already has a dragon saddle (which is possible, but also highly unlikely), you will need to craft your own. A block of wood makes a good base on which to sit, once it has been carved to fit you. Cover the wood with sturdy fabric or leather. Leather is also a good, strong material for the straps. Present the saddle to your dragon as at gift.

The front of the saddle is higher than the saddle itself. This is for grabbing hold, especially when the dragon goes into a dive.

Rings of iron hold the strap to the saddle.

The buckle is fastened beneath the dragon's belly.

When I first rode the gold dragon Auren's back, I didn't have the luxury of a saddle. Instead I had to hang on tight to his scales so I wouldn't fall off as we soared over stormy ocean waves. I thought it was wonderfully challenging and fun, but my companions were terrified. They say the only way to ride a dragon is with a well-crafted saddle.

Dragons as Mounts

Training your dragon takes six weeks of hard work and energy—from both you and your dragon. Your dragon must become familiar with the saddle, and it must understand what you want it to do.

The main thing you must keep in mind when training your dragon as a mount is respect. You must remember at all times that dragons are highly intelligent and independent creatures. I know I've already written about this, but I cannot stress it enough.

Here are some dos and don'ts for training your dragon to be a mount:

Dragon Dos

DO have patience. Dragons learn quickly, but because your dragon is young, it will make mistakes.

DO reward your dragon, but keep the reward modest. Dragons don't like to feel that they are being bribed or bargained with. You might give your dragon its favorite food or a small treasure, but don't overdo it.

DO treat your dragon with respect!

DO praise your dragon.

DO allow your dragon to rest and have time to, well, to be a dragon. Training and schooling all the time will only frustrate your dragon. Let your dragon express its natural personality.

Dragon Don'ts

DON'T talk down or insult your dragon. Remember that your dragon is intelligent!

DON'T criticize your dragon too harshly. You must remember that your dragon is doing you a favor. It doesn't need to be your mount. It can simply leave whenever it feels like it. If you constantly scold your dragon, it will stop listening and obeying.

DON'T use any spells or charms to get your dragon to follow your instructions. Once the spell wears off, the dragon will no longer obey, and you will have wasted precious time.

DON'T train your dragon for purposes that the dragon is opposed to. For example, if you are training a dragon so you can more easily hunt, don't choose a gold dragon as your mount. A gold dragon will not want to harm living things. Therefore, it will not take kindly to being trained. And most important of all . . .

DON'T forget that your dragon is a DRAGON!

I can tell you from experience that kind words go a long way, my friends! My old mentor, Maddoc, was reluctant to give praise. However, when he did, my spirits soared.

You'd be surprised at the mistake would-be dragon riders make when they start treating their dragon as if it were a rambunctious puppy. Dragons are unique, wise, and wonderful. Don't forget!

Communicating with a Dragon

One of the skills that will help you to train and ride your dragon is communication. Dragons can, indeed, understand our language. However, your dragon will bond with you more freely if you attempt to learn some dragon words. These words will also help if you take your dragon into battle. Your dragon will respond more quickly to words in its own language than in your own.

the language of dragons

I learned Draconic as an apprentice to the wizard Maddoc. But whether you are an apprentice or not, if you wish to become a dragon rider, you will need to know these words. The spelling of the words might look odd and seem even harder to say. That is why you must practice them.

Believe me, it took me quite some time to learn Draconic words, but once I did, it greatly helped my relationships with dragons like Auren.

Common	Draconic		Common	Draconic
above	svern		mountain	verthicha
after	ghent		name	ominak
and	vur		near	leirith
bag	waeth		no	thrice
before	ghoros		ogre	ghontix
behind	zara		on	shafear
beside	unsiti		rain	oposs
but	shar		red	charir
demon	kothar		rest	ssifisv
die	loreat		shadow	sjach
dwarf	tundar		skin	molik
elf	vaecaesin		small	kosj
enemy	irlym		smart	othokent
evil	malsvir		so	zyak
far	karif		soar	hysvear
forest	caesin		song	miirik
flee	osvith		sorceror	vorastrix
fly	austrat		storm	kespek
friend	thurirl		through	erekess
gem	kethend		travel	ossalur
give	majak		under	onureth
gnome	terunt		valley	arux
go	gethrisj		want	tuor
gold	aurix		war	aryte
green	achuak		water	hesjing
home	okarthel		we	yth
human	munthrek		white	aussir
in	persvek		yes	axun
many	throden		you	wux

Learning words in Draconic does more than help you communicate with your dragon. It shows your dragon that you are committed to your partnership. After all, if your dragon must learn your language, then you should learn its language too.

When trying to speak these words, stress the first syllable. When I practice the language, I include Draconic words in my everyday speech. For example, suppose you want to tell your dragon to fly. You could say:

Austrat, darastrix! Austrat! Darastrix is Draconic for dragon.

If you wanted to tell your dragon where to fly, you could say:

Gethrisj leirith verthicha! Can you figure out what this means?

Caring for a Dragon

Caring for your dragon shows your loyalty and respect for such a noble creature. Dragons are independent creatures. They certainly don't need you to see to their welfare. But by allowing you to ride it, the dragon is in essence doing you a favor. In return, you must provide it with treasure, shelter, and food. The kind of treasure, shelter, and food you need depends on the dragon you choose to have a relationship with.

Dragon Treasure

Dragons are collectors by nature, and each dragon collects—or hoards—something different. That is why if you wish to keep a dragon, you must also provide the dragon with the treasure of its choice. No one knows exactly why dragons crave treasure. Some say it is instinct. Others guess it relates to their high intelligence and ability to recognize value and beauty. Whatever the reason, all dragons enjoy boasting about the size and value of their hoard. To maintain good relations with your dragon, be prepared for lengthy discussions of your dragon's loot.

Dragon Lair

If you have decided to raise or partner with a dragon, you must provide your dragon with a lair. You can't expect a dragon to live with you, no matter how humble or grand your abode might be. Your dragon's lair shouldn't be just any convenient location. (After all, a dragon is not just any creature!) You must accommodate your dragon in the type of place that the dragon is most accustomed to, and that might not be as easy as it at first seems. Dragons are not found in the common village or local meadow. You must duplicate the conditions of your particular dragon's lair.

Be sure the treasure you offer suits the exact kind of dragon you ride! No dragon will accept any item of value. They each have particular tastes. If you can't remember which kind of treasure your dragon likes best, refer to A Practical Guide to Dragons.

Dragon Food

An excellent way to bond with your dragon is to share a meal, especially if it is one that you have brought to your dragon. But here are a few extra special delights you can share with your dragon to ensure its loyalty for life:

BLACK:

Catch some tasty fish, a scallop, or other treat from the sea. It's the perfect way to bond with this notoriously grouchy dragon.

BLUE:

Blue dragons enjoy tasty morsels they find in the desert, such as snakes and other reptiles. They'll also eat desert plants if meat is scarce.

GREEN:

You might not feel comfortable feeding them what they like best—sprites and elves! So train your green dragon to dine only on plants.

RED:

Red dragons love meat. Sharing a slice of tender beef or chicken with your red dragon wyrmling is sure to endear this nasty, feisty creature to you.

WHITE:

The best way to this dragon's heart is to freeze its food. Let the dragon watch you unfreeze it to show how dedicated you are to its care.

Bear in mind, reds love to eat female humans and elves. Keep this in mind when selecting a dragon to ride!

BRASS:

Dew drops, so rare in the desert (the brass dragon's natural habitat), are sure to be an extra special treat.

BRONZE:

These dragons are particularly fond of shark meat. They love to feast on these carnivores of the sea.

COPPER:

Copper dragons adore scorpions and other venomous creatures.

GOLD:

Gold dragons adore pearls and gemstones. Unless you have unlimited funds at your disposal to buy these, you may want to think twice about partnering with a gold dragon.

SILVER:

The silver dragon will enjoy a meal with you, no matter what you eat. A silver dragon is probably the easiest of the dragons to feed.

If you want to know more about dragon diets, you'll need to pull out A Practical Guide to Dragons.

RIDING A DRAGON

You've raised your dragon, you've trained it, you've formed a bond with it by caring for it. You have the proper saddle, and you've even learned a few choice words in Draconic. Now, my friends, it is time for you to climb aboard your dragon and take your first flight. *How exhilarating!*

As you've probably already noticed, your dragon is not very tall. Oh, it can be, if it is standing on its back legs! But a dragon's legs are not very long compared to the rest of its body. In fact, they can be rather short. To perch on the back of your dragon is not that difficult.

Because a dragon's legs are rather stubby, their legs are not very powerful. A dragon can take off from the ground, with a little help from its tail. The ideal spot, however, for you to experience your first dragon flight is from a hill or the edge of a rocky cliff. Then your dragon can simply swoop down and up, its wings flapping gloriously as you lift off into the air together. *Spectacular! You have now become a dragon rider!*

Follow these directions, which I translated from the Draconic book I found in Maddoc's tower.

HOW TO SIT ASTRIDE YOUR DRAGON

1. Grab tightly to the strap of the saddle.
2. Pull yourself up along the dragon's back.
3. Lift one leg over the saddle.
4. Settle your backside into the saddle.
5. Hold firmly to the front of the saddle.

You should now be seated quite nicely on the back of your dragon.

Dragon Movements

Whether on land, underground, in the sea, or in the air, a dragon exhibits amazing speed and grace of movement.

In Flight

A dragon, obviously, is most comfortable flying through the air. What can you expect from your dragon in flight? First, you must know that a dragon does not move its wings very quickly, as you might have seen birds do. Instead, the wing movement is slow and steady.

When flying, a dragon attempts to keep its body as straight as possible. It extends its neck, tail, and hind legs, and tucks its front legs up beneath its chest.

If you recall, you will not be steering your dragon, but rather, your dragon will be steering itself.

Dragons move at different speeds depending on their size. If you wish to select your mount based on how quickly (or slowly!) it moves, the following chart of maximum speeds may prove useful. (Remember an average human walks at only about two to three miles per hour.)

Dragon Type	Walk (miles per hour)	Fly (miles per hour)	Swim (miles per hour)	Burrow (miles per hour)
Black dragon	360	900	360	—
Blue dragon	300	1200	—	180
Brass dragon	360	1500	—	180
Bronze dragon	240	1500	360	—
Copper dragon	240	1500	—	—
Gold dragon	360	1500	360	—
Green dragon	240	1200	240	—
Red dragon	240	1200	—	—
Silver dragon	240	1200	—	—
White dragon	360	1500	360	180

One disadvantage that dragons have, especially when fighting in battle, is that they cannot make quick and sudden moves. Their strong, graceful bodies turn slowly when in flight. Dragons also make wide circles when flying.

The dragon changes direction by moving its neck and tail, similar to the way a fish moves through water. The dragon can also use the frills along its back to help change direction.

A dragon can coast like this for hours!

By Land, By Sea

When a dragon moves along the ground, it walks much like a cat, lifting one front foot and the opposite hindfoot at the same time. When walking, the dragon's wings stay folded at its sides. A tired or old dragon may allow its tail to drag along the ground. But most of the time, the tail stays raised, gently moving from side to side to help the dragon maintain its balance.

All dragons can swim, however black, green, white, bronze, and gold dragons are best suited to undersea adventure as they can breathe underwater. When underwater, a dragon folds its wings in and throws its legs back. It glides through the water in an almost snake-like fashion, by weaving its body in a side-to-side motion and lashing its tail back and forth.

A dragon burrows by using its head and front claws to dig into the soil, then kicking away the piles of dirt with its back legs. While all dragons can dig small holes, only blue, white, and brass dragons can burrow successfully. Their thick necks, stocky legs, and wedge-shaped heads allow them to tunnel through the ground with ease.

While graceful in flight, most dragons have a rather stocky, lumbering gait.

Swimming dragons can bear a rider, while burrowing dragons will not.

No Space Too Small

As you fly with your dragon, you might come across narrow gorges, canyons, and rocky crevices. You'll wonder if you and your dragon will make it. But do not worry! Dragons can fold their wings against their bodies and glide right through.

No Tricky Moves

Dragons are not known for making tricky moves. If they need to, they can execute a somersault to quickly change direction. They can also hover slightly, but not for long. While hovering, the dragon can move its body up or down. I don't know if you'd call that tricky, but it might come in handy during battle!

Unless its has no other choice, a dragon prefers a leisurely pace. It would rather walk than run, and in flight, it loves to coast from one updraft to another. All the better for the rider, I say!

Dragon Abilities

Dragons have many abilities that are unique to their species, from their fine-tuned senses of hearing, sight, and smell to their incredible strength and speed. But none of their abilities are as amazing to me as their skills in casting magic.

You don't need to train your dragon to do magic. It just naturally can. Magic is an innate skill, one the dragon doesn't need to practice in order to perform. When called upon, the dragon's magic emerges. This can be especially useful if you and your dragon are in battle.

I once saw a gold dragon creating a magical sunburst, like this one. It was an amazing sight to behold!

Dragons have been known to acquire magic items and create potions to augment their already powerful magical abilities!

I've long known dragons were capable of magic, but when I was in Maddoc's tower practicing my Draconic, I translated this document which shows the unique magical abilities each type of dragon possesses.

Dragon Type	Special Magical Abilities
Black dragon	Create darkness Summon plagues of insects Accelerate plant growth
Blue dragon	Throw voice like a ventriloquist Create mirages
Brass dragon	Speak with animals Control wind and weather
Bronze dragon	Speak with animals Create food and water Make fog Control water and weather Detect thought
Copper dragon	Take the shape of stone Change rock to mud, or mud to rock Create walls of stone Move earth
Gold dragon	See the future Create sunbursts
Green dragon	Accelerate plant growth Command plants Dominate people
Red dragon	Locate hidden paths Locate lost objects
Silver dragon	Create fog Control the wind and weather Reverse gravity
White dragon	Create fog Create gusts of wind Create walls of ice Control weather

Some dragons have horns atop their heads that can cause quite severe wounds.

Don't forget the dragon's sharp teeth and strong jaws! You wouldn't want to be on the biting end of an angry dragon!

Dragons don't often use their claws, but the claws are still sharp and can cause quite a bit of damage.

The dragon's long neck helps it strike out at enemies.

Dragon Defenses

Dragons are naturally equipped with weapons and armor. The dragon's scales are nearly impossible to penetrate. The way they overlap, combined with the strong muscles beneath, make the dragon nearly invulnerable.

A dragon's breath weapon can be deadly

The dragon's main weapon is its breath weapon. All dragons breathe an element that can harm or hinder others, but they also often use their wit and intelligence to defeat a foe. Dragons can also strike such fear that their foes cannot move or speak, let alone fight. This ability is called dragonfear.

I have never felt the power of dragonfear because kender don't feel fear. But it sounds amazing!

The sharp, pointy tip of the dragon's wings can also rip and tear.

Watch out for the tail! It can whip and snap and cause incredible injury.

Dragon Weaknesses

Dragons have very few weaknesses. Their very presence alone can render fear. Yet dragons can be vulnerable, especially to conditions opposite of what they are used to. For example, a red dragon cannot be harmed by fire or heat, but it can become weak when exposed to the cold and snow.

Dragon Rider Defenses

When riding a dragon, you may be called upon to take your dragon into battle. You and your dragon are perfect combatants, especially with the proper defenses.

This armor was made from the hide of a red dragon, so the armor will repel the fire of a red dragon.

Dragonhide Armor

Dragonhide armor doesn't have many magical qualities, but it does have one major benefit: It can repel the breath weapon of the same type of dragon from which the dragonhide was made.

The best way to protect your body during battle is to wear protective armor, especially armor made from dragonhide. You will need to visit a blacksmith, a person who creates armor. Explain your need for dragonhide armor and the fact that you are a dragon rider. (Say it proudly!) The blacksmith will create body armor specifically for your body. After all, you wouldn't want your lifesaving armor to be too big or too tight, would you? That would not help you in battle, now, would it?

Dragonlance

The dragonlance is a very special weapon designed to kill a dragon. Yes, I know, it is harsh to hear, and even harder to have to use. But the time may arise when evil dragons threaten you and the ones you love. Then you must do what you can to save your village, and the dragonlance is the most deadly of weapons. Dragonlances are also not easy to obtain. You must earn the right to wield a dragonlance. Your connection with your dragon, combined with your pure conviction to your task, will supply the dragonlance you might so desperately need.

It's the true weapon of a dragon rider!

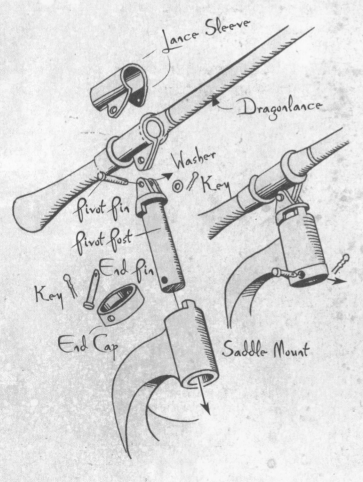

Lance Sleeve

Dragonlance

Washer

Key

Pivot Pin

Pivot Post

Key

End Pin

End Cap

Saddle Mount

Dragonlance Mount

Your dragon saddle has no place to store your dragonlance. This diagram shows an adequate dragonlance mount to be attached to the saddle. Notice how the weapon slips snugly into the sleeve, which sits perpendicular to the mounting apparatus. The dragonlance sits comfortably at your side and remains available when needed.

Dragoncraft Defenses

Dragoncraft are items made from the parts of a dragon. They have no magic in and of themselves. But because they are crafted from a dragon's body, they are very strong and durable. Just imagine holding a weapon made from a dragon! It's as if the dragon's power lies dormant, and it springs to life when you put the item into use.

Dragoncraft! Don't you just love the sound of that word? It gave me shivers the first time I heard the wizard Maddoc say it out loud. The word conjures up all sorts of items too wondrous to behold!

Dragonhide Mantle

Dragon hide can also be used to create a cape or cloak. It adds an extra layer of protection, for although it is more fluid than body armor, it is still very strong and hard to penetrate.

A dragonhide mantle such as this one can also make a dragon rider appear more intimidating to dragons. This can be especially useful if you and your dragon must engage in combat while in flight.

Dragonbone Bow

This bow is made from dragonbone. Note the long, slender shape. It was most likely taken from the leg, or perhaps the rib or wing bone. The bone is extraordinarily strong. Although I've never used one, I'm told that an arrow shot from such a bow will travel much farther than an arrow shot from a regular bow.

Dragonfang Dagger

Don't forget the dragon's teeth and claws! They can also be used to craft weapons such as arrows and daggers. The dragonfang dagger is particularly effective when in combat. Simply showing the dagger might scare your enemy off!

A dragonfang dagger only weighs about two pounds!

Dragonhide Bracers

These are called bracers. They protect your arms in combat. Being made of dragon hide, they will make you look like you are part dragon!

Dragon Mask

The mask, made of brilliant metals and gems, resembles a dragon's head. But it has an even more useful purpose than acting as a disguise: The mask allows you to see things that are under an invisibility spell!

Imagine wearing such a thing as this! I have never encountered one, but I would love to slip one on and view the world through its eyes.

Necklace of Copper Dragon Scales

This necklace might not look like much, but it certainly can save you! The scales have the power to protect you from painful and deadly acid. Simply touch one of the scales and say a command word, and no acid can harm you. Each scale can be used only once, and when all the scales are used, the necklace has no more power. Still, it is an effective weapon when facing an acid-breathing foe.

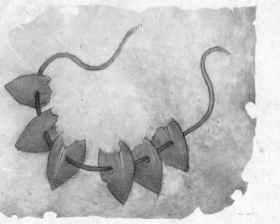

Each scale on this necklace is about the size of a small coin.

Dragon Eye Amulet

This amulet resembles the eye of a dragon! The eye, which is about the size of a fist, dangles from a heavy gold chain. The sight of such an amulet must be amazing to behold. This amulet increases the wearer's competence and confidence.

Be sure to wear this amulet on a sturdy gold chain, especially when riding your dragon. If the chain is not strong enough, this hefty amulet can break free of its chain and shatter on the ground.

Wyrmfang Amulet

This necklace doesn't have dragon scales—it has dragon teeth! The teeth hang on a strip of leather. To the outsider, the necklace might not look like much. But you know better! The necklace enhances the power of all the weapons at your disposal. It is truly a brilliant piece of dragoncraft. So if you are able to gather the teeth of a dragon and string them together, you'll have a powerful weapon in your arsenal.

I would love to feel how much more powerful my weapons could be!

DRAGONS IN COMBAT

The world of dragons is not always a peaceful one, and often dragons are called into service to help fight an enemy who desires only destruction. You and your dragon will become instrumental in such a battle, for a dragon is a fierce fighter, especially from the air.

Aerial Combat

Dragons can move swiftly on the ground, but not quite as swiftly as they can when aloft. The sight of a dragon hurtling out of the sky, wings unfurled, teeth bared, breath weapon in action is sure to send many an enemy fleeing! In combat, your dragon's breath weapon can be one of your best offensive or defensive weapons. If you wish to select a mount based on this ability, consider this chart.

Dragon Type	Breath Weapon
Black dragon	Acid
Blue dragon	Lightning
Brass dragon	Fire and sleep gas
Bronze dragon	Lightning and repulsion gas
Copper dragon	Acid and slow gas
Gold dragon	Cone of weakness and fire
Green dragon	Chlorine gas
Red dragon	Fire
Silver dragon	Paralyzing gas and cone of cold
White dragon	Frost

Dragon Rider Duties

Good dragon riders not only spend time riding and caring for their dragons, they also make sure to keep their own physical and mental skills in top form. If you wish to become a dragon rider, you must maintain an excellent sense of balance, strong legs for riding and jumping, a flexible body for tumbling, sharp eyesight, and the ability to concentrate on a task for long periods of time.

Remember: Dragons are intensely intelligent and independent creatures, with excellent eyesight. They do not require dragon riders in combat situations. However if you have done a good job of forming a bond with your dragon and if you have gained its trust and respect, your dragon will come to rely on you if ever it finds itself engaged in aerial combat. When and if this occurs, you can assist your dragon in a number of ways.

While in Maddoc's tower, I found this list of instructions as I flipped through a book of famous battles. It includes many suggestions for helping your dragon in combat.

Turning Radius

The Blind Spot

Your dragon has excellent vision, that is for sure. But your dragon does not have eyes on the back of its head. You can be your dragon's eyes. Look all around you, especially behind you. Alert your dragon of troubles you see.

Turning Radius

A dragon cannot make many sudden moves or turn in tight circles with a rider on its back. The dragon will have to bank into a turn to avoid losing the rider. If your dragon needs to turn around, it will have to make a wide circle in order to do so. You can assist your dragon in making a turn by pinpointing exactly where a dragon needs to go. Give your dragon specific directions and locations. This will improve your dragon's turning radius.

Do Some of the Work

In combat, your dragon is often in attack mode. Help your dragon along as needed. Don't wait for your dragon to take the first plunge. If you have a bow, shoot your arrows! If you have spears, throw them! If you have a dragonlance, use it!

Don't Cause Trouble

You must always remain focused when you and your dragon are in battle. Don't cause extra work or trouble for your dragon. The worst thing you can do during a battle is to fall off in midflight, causing your dragon to come after you. So sit tight and concentrate on what is happening around you.

Combat Maneuvers

You've already learned that your dragon cannot make quick, sudden moves. Even so, it can charge an enemy in frightening and effective ways.

Dive Attack

During a dive attack, the dragon will soar directly toward a target at an abnormally high speed. It will fly with its claws out, using them to wound and grab.

Fly-by Attack

A dragon might perform this action if it wants to surprise its foe. Charging at top speed, it will pause long enough to attack, and then continue flying.

Ram

Targets might not necessarily be on the ground. Sometimes an enemy will attack in midair. Then the dragon might ram the creature in flight. Because of the dragon's strength, smashing into a foe is a sure way to unseat a rider, as well as to knock the enemy off its course.

When a dragon rider chases another dragon, you typically follow three possible paths.

A lag pursuit is when your dragon flies behind the enemy dragon. Use this to catch up to the enemy dragon.

TYPES OF PURSUIT

Lag

Pure

Lead

If your dragon points directly at the enemy dragon, you are flying a pure pursuit. This is best for using your dragonlance or other closer-range weapons.

If you are heading out in front of the enemy dragon, you are on a lead pursuit. This is used to close in on the enemy dragon.

Combat Dangers

Aerial combat is thrilling and usually successful, but it can also be fraught with dangers. Your dragon is a splendid flier, but in battle, it can succumb to a few mishaps. So beware of these dangers when flying atop your dragon. With the special bond you and your dragon share, you should be able to alert your dragon if you sense a mishap about to occur.

Dragon Highlords

During the War of the Lance, a very special kind of dragon rider emerged. The Dark Queen, through treacherous means, forged an alliance with the chromatic dragons and convinced them to fight on her side. The dragons formed five armies, one for each color of dragon, and the leader of each army was called a Dragon Highlord. Dragon Highlords commanded their armies while riding a powerful dragon mount. The War of the Lance has ended, yet some say Dragon Highlords still roam the skies.

I must study more about these fascinating leaders. I have heard that the tales of the war were collected in volumes known as the Dragonlance Chronicles. I must remember to look for them in the Great Library if I ever return to Palanthas.

Stall

In order to remain in flight, a dragon must maintain a certain speed. If a dragon starts to slow down, it might stop flying altogether. This might lead to a free fall, so it is immensely important that you shout out a warning to your dragon to keep up its speed.

Free Fall

Your dragon will be very focused on the battle, so focused that it might lose its timing when flying. This might result in your dragon plunging to the ground in a free fall. Pay attention to your dragon's speed and wing movement. If you sense that your dragon's strength is waning, let your dragon know.

Other Flying Foes

Besides dragons, what other creatures with riders might attack you and your dragon in midair? During aerial combat, you might also encounter these creatures who can also take to the air with riders on their backs.

Griffon

The griffon is not half as big as a dragon, but it is a pesky creature. Griffons are about eight feet long, have the head of an eagle and the body of a lion. A griffon will swoop down for an attack, using its sharp talons and pointy beak to cause harm.

Hippogriff

These creatures are very aggressive. They're a combination of horse and eagle. They dive from above, claws extended, intending to rip and shred whatever is threatening them.

Pegasus

Although this winged horse might seem like a gentle foe, do not be fooled! The pegasus can be a fierce warrior, attacking with sharp hooves as it approaches from any direction. And beware of those sharp teeth! They have a nasty bite!

Fighting a Dragon

True dragon riders must know how to defend themselves. There may come a time in your journeys as a dragon rider where your own dragon is so injured that it cannot help you against an enemy. Even when you are not expecting combat, you must be prepared.

Not every dragon you meet will be your friend and companion. Even your own dragon can turn on you if you do not show it the respect and loyalty that it expects. If you find yourself in the path of an angry dragon, here are a few strategies. Some are taken from my own experiences, others from anecdotes I've collected during my travels.

Find a Confined Space

Dragons fight best when they have a lot of room to fly and stomp and flip their tails. If you come across a dragon in an open area, the dragon has the advantage. Your best strategy is to lure the dragon into a smaller, more confined space. This will limit the dragon's range of motion. *Just be careful not to lead the dragon back into its own lair!*

Remain Silent

It is very difficult to sneak up on a dragon. Not only do they have excellent vision, but their other senses are very acute as well. A dragon will probably sense your presence before you are aware of it. Still there are ways you can avoid contact with the dragon. If you have any magical abilities, you can cast a silence spell around yourself. This will reduce the chances of the dragon locating you.

Don't Overstay Your Welcome

This is probably the most important advice. Leave the place of battle as quickly as possible, even if it means leaving behind a valued object or piece of clothing. Hopefully, this lost trinket will appease the dragon, and it will soon forget you ever existed.

Remember, hiding in a dark lair will not ensure your safety. Dragons have excellent vision, even in the dark.

> ## WARNING!
>
> A dragon is a highly intelligent foe with unparalleled magic powers. Few magic spells will work on a dragon in combat. Even if a spell appears to take hold, the magic will quickly wear off and the dragon will be as formidable as ever. Sleep spells or paralysis spells do not work at all on any draconic creatures. And dragons barely register the blows of a standard weapon. It takes wit, wisdom, and just the right kind of weapons to succeed in a battle with a dragon.

Not to mention luck!

DRAGONKIND

The creatures on the following pages are all related to the dragon family. I have come across some in my travels, while others remain the stuff of legends. You will have to watch for them on your own adventures and discern if they are friendly and can be approached, or if you are better off leaving them be.

Ghostly Dragon

The ghostly dragon is one of the saddest of creatures. A ghostly dragon is a dragon that was killed and had its treasure taken. The dragon becomes a ghost and haunts its lair, constantly looking for its lost hoard of trinkets. Both metallic and chromatic dragons can become ghostly dragons.

Don't let the ghostly dragon's forlorn appearance fool you. If you enter a lair in which a ghostly dragon lives, the dragon is very much aware of your presence. It will lurk and watch, and then suddenly it will reveal itself. Ghostly dragons have the same breath weapon as they did when they were alive and are just as dangerous, so do not take these dragons lightly—even though they may tug at your heartstrings, as they do mine.

Restoring the dragon's stolen treasure may put the dragon to rest. It will gather up its treasure and simply disappear.

I once met the most amazing ghostly dragon named Theoran beside a fabled Dragon Well in the kingdom of Arngrim. He gave me a gift that changed my life forever and set me on the path to discovering the meaning of my amazing magical abilities.

Rust Dragon

If you come across a silver, copper, or brass dragon, and something looks a bit strange, then you might have come across a rust dragon. A rust dragon resembles its metallic counterparts from a distance. But when you get up close, you'll quickly see the differences. Instead of spectacular, shimmery scales, the scales of a rust dragon are tarnished. The rust dragon's hide appears dull and pitted with holes. They prefer to snack on iron than on living beings, so most creatures are safe from this dragon.

Rust dragons are actually very handy in battle. That's because their breath weapon destroys metal. When engulfed by the rust dragon's breath weapon, metal weaponry or metal armor will quickly erode and fall apart. The rust dragon can also shoot a line of acid.

The wings of a rust dragon are not nearly as remarkable as those of a true dragon. The skin between the bones is thin and looks barely strong enough to support it in flight.

Faerie Dragon

Combine the majesty of a dragon and the charm of the faeries, and you have one of the world's most perfect creatures! The faerie dragon is about the size of a small animal. Its size makes it perfect to romp and ally with faeries. It loves mischief, and it is a pleasure to encounter—if you can find one.

Faerie dragons may be comfortable around the faerie folk, but they are rather shy around other creatures. You might catch sight of their brilliant blue, green, and pink colors and believe you've spotted a butterfly. Its long tail waves and wags, especially when the faerie dragon is happy.

Landwyrm

According to my research, landwyrms are supposedly very similar to dragons, except for one main difference: Landwyrms lack wings! They are intelligent and clever, and they retain all sorts of knowledge about the places where they live. That, actually, is how landwyrms are categorized—by their habitat. Unlike chromatic dragons, landwyrms are not innately evil. They can actually be quite helpful because of all their knowledge. But like true dragons, they must be treated with respect.

I have never heard tell of landwyrms in our world. Maddoc swears they do not exist. But why, then, did he have an entire book on the subject hidden in his library? I intend to one day determine for sure whether these creatures can be found on Krynn.

Desert Landwyrm

This landwyrm has the most wonderful nickname—"tomb dragon." Doesn't such a name just send a shiver down your back? They get this name because they often live in old, ruined buildings in the desert, such as ancient tombs. A desert landwyrm often burrows under the desert sand, lying in wait for prey. Its sandy brown scales blend in perfectly with the desert landscape. When prey approaches, the desert landwyrm reveals itself in all its sandy colored glory, its sharp claws ready to grab. The only enemy it has is the blue dragon, and the two often clash over desert territories.

Forest Landwyrm

The forest landwyrm is a most decent and noble being. It lives in the forest and guards its forest home from enemies. These might include simple, harmless forest creatures. It does not harm them, mind you, but merely chases them off. In this way, the forest landwyrm's home remains safe and secure. Its brown and green scales help it to blend in perfectly with the forest, and you might come across one quite by accident.

Hill Landwyrm

This landwyrm is the big bully of the bunch. It enjoys taunting and intimidating creatures much smaller and weaker than itself, showing off how strong and muscular it is, and waving its deadly, sharp claws. Yet what happens when it sees a large army or a much larger creature? It runs away! The hill landwyrm is not a noble creature, that is for certain. My advice is to simply stay out of its path. Its scales vary in color and may blend in with the landscape. Look for a single row of horns atop its head to identify this creature.

If you don't want the desert landwyrm to snatch you up, you'd better quickly announce yourself as a friend, not foe!

If you do, work your hardest to prove that you are not a threat. If you are able to do so, you will have quite a treat. The forest landwyrm may invite you to sit for awhile and chat with it. I look forward to such an encounter myself!

Tylor

Tylors are very rare in our world, but I can vouch for the fact that they do exist. Their appearance is quite similar to landwyrms. Pointed horns and a pair of winglike fins protrude from the sides of their skulls. Their most amazing feature by far is that of invisibility. Tylors have skin that can be camouflaged to match their surroundings so closely that they become practically invisible. If you ever see a shimmer in the air around you, watch out! It could be a tylor waiting to pounce.

I once encountered a tylor in the desert wastelands of Khur! It was an amazing sight to witness a huge, blue-skinned creature popping out of thin air to attack our caravan. But that's another story . . .

Vampire Dragon

The voice of a vampire dragon is so compelling that it casts a spell over its victim. The vampire dragon does not need to look at its victim to cast the spell. In fact, once the spellbound victim sees the vampire dragon, it usually revives and is no longer enchanted. Vampire dragons also do not like sunlight. If exposed to the sun, their movements slow and they are less powerful. Vampire dragons hoard treasures, just as true dragons do.

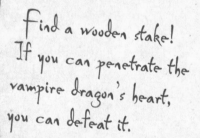

Find a wooden stake! If you can penetrate the vampire dragon's heart, you can defeat it.

These creatures are extremely rare—but I find them fascinating! Vampire dragons have many features that common vampires have, such as not casting a shadow and not making reflections in mirrors. Also, like a vampire, they suck the blood from their victims.

Zombie Dragon

Many zombie dragons are the offspring of vampire dragons. If a vampire dragon attacks and drains the blood of an adult or mature dragon, the dragon will turn into a vampire dragon. But if the vampire dragon attacks and drains the blood of a young adult or younger dragon, the dragon becomes a zombie dragon.

A zombie dragon's once beautiful hide is putrid and pocked with holes. And the stench! Zombie dragons have a most foul-smelling odor. The zombie dragon has no mind of its own, and it can only follow the most simple of instructions. For this reason, the zombie dragon is usually posted as a guard for an evil sorcerer or other nasty creature.

This skeletal dragon was created from the bones of a black dragon. How about those eyes! A smoldering red light!

Skeletal Dragon

Like vampire and zombie dragons, the skeletal dragon is among the undead. If a dragon's skeleton is discovered by a powerful spellcaster, the spellcaster can revive the skeleton, creating a skeletal dragon. The skeletal dragon has very few of the powers it had when it was alive. It cannot do magic, although it does still have its sensory abilities, such as keen eyesight. The skeletal dragon has practically no mind of its own. Instead, it takes its orders from the spellcaster who created it. So if you see a skeletal dragon, beware! A stronger power is definitely pulling the strings.

I'd be interested to learn how to create a skeletal dragon. It would be quite thrilling to control such a creature, don't you think? I bet my old mentor, Maddoc, would know how. He was always bringing animal skeletons back to life. Too bad we're not on speaking terms at the moment.

Shadow Dragon

Shadow dragons are mysterious, eerie creatures. One of their main abilities is to be able to disappear in the shadows. If you are creeping through an old castle or ruin, a shadow dragon might be present, and you would never know it—unless the shadow dragon revealed itself to you. The chances of encountering a shadow dragon are very slim, mostly because they don't inhabit the material world. Most shadow dragons that do exist were summoned by another being, such as a powerful wizard or sorcerer. Once summoned, the wizard might bind the dragon to a place. So if you meet a shadow dragon, it might not be there of its own choosing.

Dracolich

The dracolich is not a natural creature. It is created by evil, and its creation is quite complicated. Below is a set of instructions I found in one of Maddoc's spellbooks. It explains the steps necessary to create a dracolich.

—I encountered a dracolich the first time my companions and I ventured to my former mentor's keep. It was gruesome but absolutely amazing! One day I hope to try to create one myself!

TO CREATE A DRACOLICH

1. Only an evil dragon and a very powerful wizard or sorcerer can create a dracolich. The dragon and spellcaster must be in agreement that the transformation will take place.

2. Once this agreement is reached, the spellcaster concocts a special beverage called the dracolich brew.

3. The evil dragon must drink this lethal concoction.

4. The dracolich brew poisons and kills the evil dragon, releasing its spirit.

5. Upon its release, the spirit transports itself to a special container— called the phylactery—that was chosen ahead of time.

6. The spirit can now transport itself into the corpse of another dragon— even its old form. It can also transfer into any dead lizardlike creature.

7. The final step is for the corpse to accept the spirit. Once it has, the dracolich transformation is complete.

Fang Dragon

This dragon is most ferocious! One has only to look at its sharp, pointy scales and its leering, frightful grin to know that this dragon is not one to be taken lightly. Fang dragons live in the mountains where the weather is mostly warm. They will travel some distance from their lairs to find a tasty meal, but not just any creature will do. No, the fang dragon prefers to dine on the flesh of intelligent creatures—such as humans and kender! This is one dragon you definitely do not want to come across. *Although it would be thrilling to behold, I'm sure!*

This dragon does not have a breath weapon, but it does have another very tricky skill: It can imitate another creature. So if you hear a voice you recognize, yet you don't see anyone, beware! It could be a fang dragon out to trap you.

Notice the forked tail— a very rare thing for any member of dragonkind

From afar, the head resembles a dragon's, doesn't it?

Wyvern

The wyvern is a poor relation to the mighty dragon. From a distance, you might even think it to be a dragon, but take a closer look. Even though it has a long neck, wings, and a long tail, it is not quite as large or majestic. However, the biggest difference is that the wyvern has no arms. The wyvern drops from the sky and attacks prey using the talons on its feet. But the wyvern's main weapon is its tail. The end has a stinging barb that injects a poison. The wyvern grabs its prey in its talons, then swings its tail around to strike. Very effective for a creature without any arms!

Draconians

Draconians are so truly evil and horrible that I am loathe to even give them space here. But this tome would not be complete without some mention of the foul beasts. Draconians can only be formed by dark, evil magic. And the magic can only be performed on the helpless eggs of metallic dragons. After an intricate ceremony, the draconians hatch from the eggs. The draconians then serve in the dark armies, fighting against good and promoting evil.

Its wings help it to glide, but not to fly.

Kapaks have a most unusual voice, a bit soft and whiny, and they bob their heads in an odd way when they speak. Although I would not like to be bitten by one, I would love to see and hear a kapak.

Kapaks have long legs and long arms, perfect for reaching enemies in battle.

Copper Dragon Draconian (Kapak)

This creature is notorious for its lethal poison. It does not have a breath weapon like a dragon's. Instead, the kapak drools its yellow poison on its weapons, then uses those weapons in battle. The kapak's poison is also released when the kapak bites someone. The poison quickly infects and paralyzes its victim. The poison will wear off in about an hour, but in most battles, an unmoving foe makes an excellent target. Most poison victims do not survive a bite from a kapak.

Brass Dragon Draconian (Baaz)

Of all the draconians, baaz are probably the weakest, while at the same time the most common. Because baaz draconians are not very tall—only about six feet—they can often pose as humans. Wearing long robes to hide their grotesque appearance, they often sneak in among the good. It must be quite a surprise when the baaz draconians reveal themselves in all their morbid glory.

The bozak's leathery wings enable it to fly for short distances. It may stay in the air for about an hour, but rarely for longer.

Its skin is a mottled brass and green.

Small, useless wings are typical of baaz draconians.

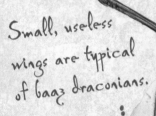

Bronze Dragon Draconian (Bozak)

Bozaks are typically not the most intelligent creatures around. Knowing they are not very brilliant, they are constantly keeping a sharp lookout for trouble. And this is what makes bozaks so useful. They make excellent leaders because they never lead their troops into battle on a whim. They take action cautiously, making sure their troops are secure. Although draconians don't have breath weapons, bozaks can create magical webs. The webs are strong enough to ensnare whatever is wrapped in them. Bozaks might cast their webs either from the air or on the ground.

Gold Dragon Draconian (Aurak)

The aurak is the most powerful of all the draconians. They have the ability to change shapes, taking on the body of a creature similar to their own size. (Auraks stand about seven feet tall.) Although they would never take the form of a kender (we are generally shorter than they would prefer, thank goodness!), they have been known to take on a human form. In this way, they lure their victims in, then ruthlessly kill them. They also have the ability to control minds. Auraks are truly an abomination, my friends. (And they smell like rotten eggs too!)

Auraks have no wings. They rarely wear clothes, but they may wear a loose-fitting cape or a belt for a sword.

Silver Dragon Draconian (Sivak)

The sivaks are a curious bunch. Evil at heart, they still make excellent warriors and would rather follow orders than give them. Sivaks are highly sought after for armies of darkness because of their one special ability. Once a sivak has killed an enemy, the sivak takes on the shape of that creature. Sivaks, standing about nine feet tall, are the largest of the draconians. They are also the only draconians that can fly endlessly, and they have the most strength. If you're not sure if a fellow among you is a sivak in disguise, take a hearty sniff. Sivaks are often accompanied by an odor of smoke and hot metal.

A sivak's wings and its powerful tail enable it to fly.

So there you have it, my friends! More practical knowledge about dragons and dragonkind. As you peruse this tome, I hope you'll gain a greater appreciation and understanding of these mythical, magical creatures, as well as a respect for them. Learning how to train and ride a dragon—and gain its respect!—can be exhausting but rewarding as well.

As for the other dragon creatures here, they must also be respected—in a different way. We must respect their powers and evil tendencies. Otherwise, we might find ourselves in their clutches. Someday I hope to meet these dragonkind and tell my own stories about them. Then I'll have to put together another guide, won't I?

Sindri

Text by

Lisa Trutkoff Trumbauer

Edited by

Nina Hess

Cover art by

Emily Fiegenschuh

Interior Art by

Daren Bader, Jino Choi, Carl Critchlow, Eric Deschamps, Wayne England,
Emily Fiegenschuh, David Hudnut, Todd Lockwood, David Martin,
Steve Prescott, Vinod Rams, Darrell Riche, Beth Trott, Anthony S. Waters,
Eva Widermann, Sam Wood

Cartography by

Shane Nitzsche

Art Direction by

Kate Irwin

Graphic Design by

Jino Choi

Don't miss these other books in the Practical Guide Family!

Visit our web site at www.mirrorstonebooks.com

A Practical Guide to Dragon Riding
© 2008 Wizards of the Coast, Inc.

Printed in the U.S.A.
First Printing: August 2008
Library of Congress Cataloging-
in-Publication Data is available
9 8 7 6 5 4 3 2
ISBN:978-0-7869-4975-5
620-21780720-001-EN

U.S., CANADA, ASIA, PACIFIC,
& LATIN AMERICA
Wizards of the Coast, Inc.
P.O. Box 707
Renton, WA 98057-0707
+1-800-324-6496

EUROPEAN HEADQUARTERS
Hasbro UK Ltd
Caswell Way
Newport, Gwent NP9 0YH
GREAT BRITIAN
Please keep this address for your records.